The Lady of Cofitachequi

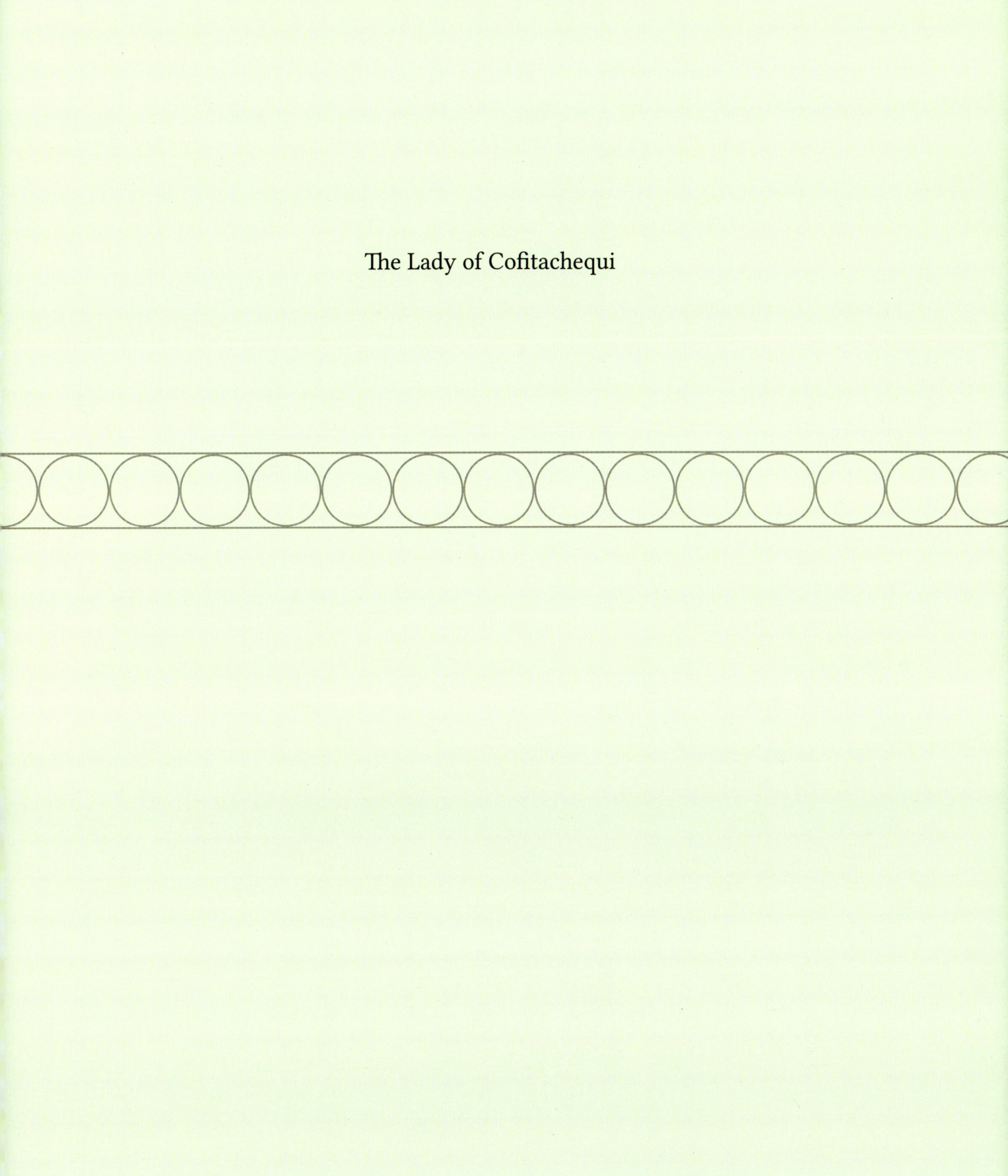

Young
Palmetto
Books

Kim Shealy Jeffcoat, Series Editor

THE LADY OF COFITACHEQUI

A South Carolina Native American Folktale

Kate Salley Palmer

Illustrated by
James H. Palmer, Jr.

THE UNIVERSITY OF
SOUTH CAROLINA PRESS

© 2019 University of South Carolina
Illustrations © James H. Palmer, Jr., 2019

Published by the University of South Carolina Press
Columbia, South Carolina 29208

www.sc.edu/uscpress

Manufactured in Korea

28 27 26 25 24 23 22 21 20 19
10 9 8 7 6 5 4 3 2 1

Library of Congress Cataloging-in-Publication Data
can be found at http://catalog.loc.gov/.

ISBN: 978-1-61117-989-7 (hardback)
ISBN: 978-1-61117-992-7 (ebook)

To Leo and Emma—KSP

To native people in South Carolina and beyond —JHP

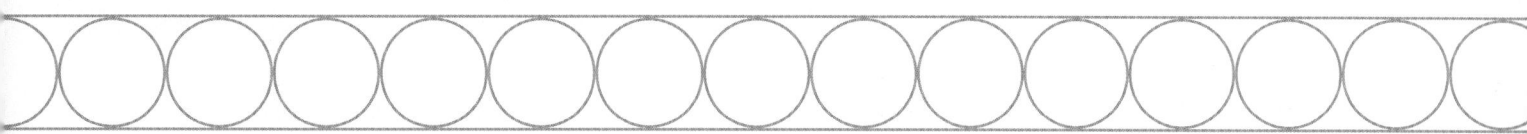

Human people lived at the riverside where the otter people had their home. Every day, the tall, two-legged humans swam with Otter and his friends. The human people washed themselves in the water and smoothed the oil of sunflower seeds onto their skin and into their shining black hair.

The Lady and her kinpeople swam in the river. Otter and his family loved the Lady. She sang like the wind and the water. The human people loved the Lady, too, for she knew the answers to many questions, and was kind to those who made mistakes. She laughed, and others laughed with her. She didn't have to be beautiful, but she was.

Otter was happy and proud that the Lady and her relations called themselves the Otter Clan. People of the Bear Clan, the Eagle Clan, and the Wolf Clan swam in the river as well. But the Lady of the Otter Clan was special.

The human people were as busy as Otter's people. The women gathered river cane and used it to make tightly woven mats to cover the roofs and walls of their temple and their dwellings. They made twine from the inner bark of trees that grew near Otter's home. They planted and tended fields of crops to feed themselves, and they wove baskets.

They made pottery from slick river clay, which they shaped and set to dry in the sun. Then they placed the pottery into special hot ovens to make it strong.

The men built dwellings from straight young trees that they felled by the riverside. Otter's friend, Beaver, boasted that it was Beaver's ancestors who had taught humans that skill. Men carried basket after basket of red, white, and black dirt to the area where they built the high place. The wise old otters said that it took many men and many seasons to build the high place, with its steep, tall sides, and flat top.

On top of the high place, the people built their temple. The temple, Otter heard, was much bigger than the dwellings. The temple walls were woven with reeds and covered with clay like those of the dwellings. Many fine, tightly woven mats covered the roof and the walls inside. But Otter knew little else about the temple. He heard the people talking and learned that it was a place where they kept the bodies of important human people who had died. Otter saw men carrying chests to the top, and he knew it was true.

At times, Otter could see a fire's glow, and hear the music of drums, voices, and dancing feet, but he could not see what happened on top of the high place.

Otter's elders told him that human people had lived by the river as long as otters had lived in the river, which was a long, long time—before the memory of any living otter.

Many four-legged people, such as Deer, Rabbit, and Wolf, came to the river to drink. Feathered people came as well, as the birds loved to sing in the trees and eat seeds from the ground.

The human people hunted many of these four-legged or feathered people for food and winter garments. The deer people and others knew this. They had seen humans show respect and ask the pardon of whomever they had just captured.

Human people needed the skin of the deer to make garments and shoes. They carved the antlers into many sharp points for the arrows they used in their hunting. They cooked the meat slowly on a rack over a fire. Sometimes they dried the meat so it would last longer and hunters could take it with them and eat from it while they were away.

Colorful feathers became beautiful garments. Other feathers helped arrows fly straighter, or adorned the hair of the human people.

As the humans prepared to plant their crop of maize one year, Otter heard Beaver's tail slap the water in warning. Otter lifted his head, and sniffed the air. There were new, strange smells on the warm breeze from across the river. Otter turned to see what new thing had entered his world.

As he turned toward the new smells, Otter could see the Lady through the trees. She wore a white garment and sat on a litter covered with white cloth. A long rope of small pearls lay around her lovely neck.

Men from the town carried the litter
on their shoulders toward the riverbank,
where several canoes awaited the people of the town. The Lady stepped
into a canoe lined with fine mats
and shaded with an awning.
Many oarsmen pulled other
canoes toward a sand-
bar across the river.

Otter stared. At the sandbar, he saw a large group of pink-skinned human people. Some of them had hair the color of nuts—or as yellow as kernels of maize! Hair sprouted from their faces. Dark hair, light hair, and hair the color of red earth stood under their noses and covered their chins.

The hairy new humans sat upon the backs of the largest four-legged people Otter had ever seen. These people had short, sleek fur, much like Otter's. Some of them were brown as tree bark, some were dark as midnight. They had huge heads and wore long straps between their giant teeth, which the hairy humans clutched. The large four-legged people were not free to wander—they had to obey the straps held by the humans.

The hairy, pink-skinned humans wore long sticks attached at their waists. These sticks lay beside their legs and moved as they moved. Hard outer shells over soft garments covered their chests and backs. The soft garments were neither the skin of deer nor the feathers of birds. The strange new humans wore curved, shiny headdresses.

Traveling with the strangers were others who looked like the Lady's human people. They wore soft garments like the ones worn by the hairy, pink-skinned people. They spoke to the pink-skinned people in a language that Otter had never heard before.

Otter listened as the hairy people spoke with one another. Then the humans who looked like the Lady's people spoke with the hairy ones. They all waited there on the sand bar, talking with one another while the large four-legged people bent their huge heads to drink from the river.

Two of the new humans stepped out to greet the Lady as her canoe landed. One was a hairy, pink-skinned stranger with a shiny curved headdress. The other looked like the Lady's people. He wore soft deerskin. The hairy stranger spoke first, in a language that Otter did not understand. Then, the human in deerskin spoke. He spoke the language of the Lady and her people.

"This man is the explorer Hernando de Soto from the country of Spain," explained the interpreter in soft deerskin. "The explorer de Soto greets you."

The Lady rose in her white garment and pearls, stepping out of the canoe.

"I am the Lady of Cofitachequi," she told the hairy stranger. "Do you come in peace or war?"

The explorer listened as the interpreter repeated the Lady's question in his language. After hearing the explorer's reply, the interpreter turned to the Lady and said, "We come in peace."

"We welcome you," said the Lady. "You and your people may stay with us as long as you like."

The interpreter told de Soto what the Lady had said, and he bowed to her.

The Lady then took the rope of pearls from around her neck and placed it around the neck of the explorer with the shiny helmet. He looked at the pearls. He spoke to the interpreter, who asked the Lady if she had more pearls like that. "Yes, she laughed, there are more than your horses can carry." The explorer de Soto seemed happy when the interpreter told him what the Lady had said.

Otter saw that the people of the town were preparing to welcome the visitors. First, the people of the town made rafts to ferry the strangers across the river. Then they made several dwellings ready for the strangers to use, laying mats and deerskin on the benches and making beds inside. Otter saw preparations for activity on the high place. He saw basket after basket of food being carried to the top. He saw the people dressing and painting themselves for a special ceremony.

When the strange-looking humans arrived in the village, the townspeople gathered around them. The people offered wild turkeys, maize, and dried fruits to the strangers. The people of the town were curious about the clothing the strangers wore, the sticks they carried, and the large-headed giants upon which they rode.

That night, the high place glowed with firelight and pulsated with the rhythm of drums and dancing feet. Beautiful songs, telling the story of the people, drifted down to the ears of Otter.

In the days that followed, the interpreter in soft deerskin was very busy. His job was to tell the people of the town what the strangers were saying. Then he told the strangers what the townspeople said. There was much talk and many questions from both sides.

The strangers asked about precious metals called gold and silver. They said they had been told that the Lady and her people had these precious metals. The Lady and her people told the strangers over and over again that there was no gold or silver in the village, and that the people did not know where to find them.

The strangers asked about precious gems as well. They wanted stones they called emeralds and rubies, sapphires and diamonds. But the people of the town had no such gems. The only precious items they had were the pearls that lay strung around their necks and upon the roof of their council house. Pearls lay buried with their dead in the buildings on the high place as well.

The strangers filled many sacks with pearls that they planned to take away.

But the strangers became impatient and angry that they were unable to find precious metals and gems. They told the Lady and her people that they believed the people were hiding these things from the explorer and his men.

Otter knew that the Lady and her people would have gladly shared any metals and gems with the explorer de Soto if they had had them. It was the way of the people to be generous to visiting leaders of other tribes.

But they had no gold, no silver, and no precious gems to give.

When de Soto and his men could find no precious stones or metal, they prepared to leave. They demanded that the Lady give them men to carry their burdens and women to have as wives. The people were afraid of the strangers then. They did not want to go.

Otter's heart quivered in fear when he saw the strangers grab the Lady and force her to go with them! People of the town tried to stop the strangers, but they were fierce and pushed the people back. So the explorer de Soto and his men rode away upon the giants with big heads, making the Lady and other townspeople trudge along beside them.

Otter watched with tears of sorrow in his eyes until the last branch hid the Lady from view.

His Lady was gone. He was afraid he would never see her again, or hear her sing like the wind and the water. He was very sad.

The people of the town were sad, too. Slowly, they set to right the things that were out of place. They swept out their homes and relit their fires. They worked in the fields, for the maize was growing and needed to be tended. They planted beans and pumpkins. They hunted for birds, rabbits, and deer to feed themselves.

Slowly, the men of the town began to play games again, with their sticks and polished stones. Once more, the high place glowed with light and vibrated with activity.

The trees grew thick with leaves and the wind turned to blow from the West as the crops grew and ripened in the fields. Babies learned to walk unsteadily as Otter watched the town and longed for the Lady of the Otter Clan.

The time came for the Green Corn Ceremony. The townspeople harvested the ripened maize and placed it in large baskets. Hunters took their bows and arrows into the woods and meadows. The people boiled the nuts they had saved since the last harvest. They began to prepare the food, but they didn't eat it. They put out the fires in the council house and in their homes. They were waiting until the time was right.

Otter knew that after a time, they would eat, and they did. The people dressed for the Ceremony and relit the fires in their homes. They danced and sang, celebrating the harvest of the maize. Then they feasted on the maize as well as the meat of the deer and turkey. They ate squash from the fields and persimmon from the woods. They used the oil of nuts to flavor their stews, and they baked acorn loaves.

The people used this time to settle quarrels and forgive injustice. Most of the Ceremony happened on the high place where Otter couldn't see, but he heard the people talking as they swam in the river. The Green Corn Ceremony was a time of renewal for the people.

But the Lady wasn't there, so a bit of sadness dampened their spirits. Otter remembered other Green Corn Ceremonies, when the Lady walked tall through the town, wearing her finery for the dancing with feathers and shells in her shining hair.

After the Ceremony, life in the town settled down as the people tended the rest of their crops.

The wind changed again and trees slowly lost their green. Pumpkins had begun to ripen in the fields, and people stayed busy gathering nuts from the forest.

Otter was chasing his tail in the river when something caught his attention. What was it? Feeling a difference in the air, he lifted his head. He didn't hear anything at first. He climbed a rock and sniffed the breeze, his ears twitching. Then it came to him—a sound from long ago. A forgotten lullaby. It was a voice that sounded like the wind and the water.

The Lady of the Otter Clan! He could hear her, but he couldn't see her. People from the town lifted their heads to listen. They heard it, too.

The branches of the forest parted, and she came into view. The Lady was home! The people of the town ran to touch her and murmur their welcome. They raised their voices in a joyous song, or many joyous songs. The Lady smiled and laughed and said she was glad to be back. There was someone with the Lady—a tall human who looked like the hunters of the Lady's town. He stood quietly, holding his bow by his side. The Lady turned to him and said that this was her new husband. She said they had escaped the explorer de Soto's army together.

Otter was so happy. He swam in circles and jumped out of the water, only to dive deep and jump out again. He tired himself out with joyful circling and jumping.

That night, the sky glowed with light from the high place, and the air vibrated with the sounds of singing voices and dancing feet. The celebration lasted all night long.

The next morning, the Lady came to the river to bathe and swim. Otter swam closer to her than he ever had before, and she reached out and touched his wet fur. "Hello, Otter," she whispered.